TORNADO HITS!

Hilde Cracks the Case

HAVE YOU READ ALL THE MYSTERIES?

scholastic.com/hilde

Hilde Cracks the Case

TORNADO HITS!

BY HILDE LYSIAK
WITH MATTHEW LYSIAK

ILLUSTRATED BY
JOANNE LEW-VRIETHOFF

SCHOLASTIC INC.

To Sharlene Martin and Katie Carella.
Without your help, these cases would certainly not be cracked.

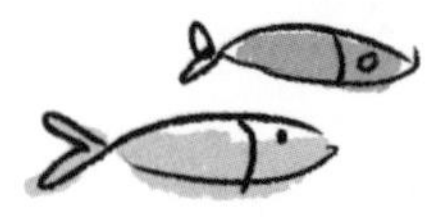

Jacket photos © Dreamstime: Kavee Pathomboon, Frbird; _human/Thinkstock.
Hilde's photo courtesy of Isabel Rose Lysiak.

Photos ©: cover spirals and throughout: Kavee Pathomboon/Dreamstime; back cover Hilde: Isabel Rose Lysiak; back cover paper: Frbird/Dreamstime; back cover tape: _human/Thinkstock; back cover paper clip: Picsfive/Dreamstime; 88 paper clips and throughout: Fosin2/Thinkstock; 88 pins: Picsfive/Dreamstime; 88 bottom: Courtesy of Joanne Lew-Vriethoff; 88 background: Leo Lintang/Dreamstime.

Library of Congress Cataloging-in-Publication Data

Names: Lysiak, Hilde, 2006- author. | Lysiak, Matthew, author. | Lew-Vriethoff, Joanne, illustrator. | Lysiak, Hilde, 2006- Hilde cracks the case ; 5. Title: Tornado hits! / by Hilde Lysiak, with Matthew Lysiak ; illustrated by Joanne Lew-Vriethoff. Description: First edition. | New York, NY : Branches/Scholastic Inc., 2018. | Series: Hilde cracks the case ; 5 | Summary: After a small tornado hits Selinsgrove during a night-time thunderstorm, Hilde and her sister/photographer, Izzy, wake up to find fish flopping all over Orange Street, and they set out to document the path of minor destruction for their newspaper—and solve the mystery of where the fish came from. Identifiers: LCCN 2018002080 | ISBN 9781338266771 (pbk) | ISBN 9781338266788 (hjk) Subjects: LCSH: Tornadoes—Juvenile fiction. | Tornado damage—Juvenile fiction. | Reporters and reporting—Juvenile fiction. | Fishes—Juvenile fiction. | Detective and mystery stories. | CYAC: Mystery and detective stories. | Tornadoes—Fiction. | Reporters and reporting—Fiction. | Fishes—Fiction. | GSAFD: Mystery fiction. | LCGFT: Detective and mystery fiction.

Classification: LCC PZ7.1.L97 To 2018 | DDC 813.6 [Fic] —dc23
LC record available at https://lccn.loc.gov/2018002080

10 9 8 7 6 5 4 3 2 1 18 19 20 21 22

Printed in China 62
First edition, October 2018
Edited by Katie Carella
Book design by Baily Crawford

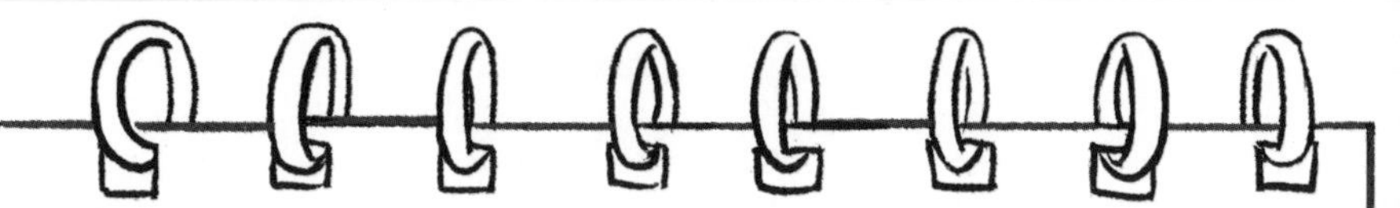

Table of Contents

1 Grove Grocer

2 Selinsgrove Forest

3 Kind Kat Café

4 Walter's Books

5 Selinsgrove University

6 Grove Pond

7 Rotary Park

Hilde's house

Introduction

Hi! My name is Hilde. (It rhymes with *build-y*!) I may be only nine years old, but I'm a serious reporter.

I learned all about newspapers from my dad. He used to be a reporter in New York City! I loved going with him to the scene of the crime. Each story was a puzzle. To put the pieces together, we had to answer six questions: Who? What? When? Where? Why? How? Then we'd solve the mystery!

I knew right away I wanted to be a reporter. But I also knew that no big newspaper was going to hire a kid. Did I let that stop me? Not a chance! That's why I created a paper for my hometown: the *Orange Street News*.

Now all I needed were stories that would make people want to read my paper. I wasn't going to find those sitting at home! Being a reporter means going out and hunting down the news. And there's no telling where a story will take me . . .

Evidence: something that helps prove if a theory is true

Interview: to talk to someone to get information

Investigate: to dig deeper into a story

Notepad: where a reporter keeps clues, quotes, and important notes

Persistence: not giving up even when a job gets difficult

Phenomenon: an unusual or extraordinary event

Press Pass: a photo ID worn by reporters

Source: a person who gives information to a reporter

Theory: an idea that hasn't been proven yet

Witness: a person who sees something happen

1 A Fishy Clue

"Hilde, wake up! Something fishy is happening on Orange Street!"

I opened my eyes. It was my older sister, Izzy. She was standing over me, shaking my arm.

"Okay, okay," I said, rubbing my eyes. "But this had better be good. The thunder from last night's storm kept me up late."

I was tired. Last night, we were with Professor Henry. He teaches at Selinsgrove University and he had been showing us how his weather-balloon drone works. The drone could track wind speeds and temperatures and do other cool stuff. But then Professor Henry's drone saw a big storm coming to Selinsgrove, and he ran off to investigate. Izzy and I had wanted to follow him, but Dad had made us go home and go to bed.

I sat up. "What is so important that it can't wait?" I asked my sister.

"This could be the most awesome news story ever! Look!" said Izzy.

I walked over to the window. It was early. The sun had not come all the way up yet. And everything looked wet from the storm.

"I don't see anything," I said.

"Look closer, down on the street," she said.

Then I saw them. All of them!

2 A Flipping, Flopping Frenzy!

At least a dozen small fish were spread out all over Orange Street. They were flipping and flopping around in large rain puddles.

I quickly got dressed.

"Izzy, how did *fish* end up in the middle of our street?" I asked as I put on my shoes.

"I don't know, but we need to go help them right away! Fish can't breathe for long out of water!" she said.

"Dad has two fishing nets in the garage. We can use them to collect the fish," I said.

"Great idea. But where are we going to put the fish once we pick them up?" she asked.

"I'm not sure," I said. "But let's figure that out *after* we get them safely off the road."

Izzy ran from my room in a blur.

I grabbed my tote bag — which had my notepad, pen, and cell phone in it. On my way downstairs, I thought about Officer Pam. Officer Pam was a wildlife officer. She always had answers when it came to animals. I sent her a quick text.

I rushed outside. Izzy was already scooping up fish in the street.

"Hurry, Hilde!" she said. "We need to get these fish into water."

First, I tried to grab a fish with my hand. But it was slimy and squished through my fingers. It fell back down to the road.

"These fish are slippery!" I said.

Izzy handed me the other net. "Don't try picking them up with your hands," she said. "Remember what Dad showed us on our fishing trips? Use the net to *scoop* the fish up."

"Oh, yeah," I said. On fishing trips, my attention was usually focused on Dad's tasty snacks. Not on Dad's nature lessons.

Scooping up the fish was a lot easier than picking them up with my hands. Soon, both of our nets were almost full!

"Did we get all the fish?" I asked.

"I think so," Izzy replied. "Now what?"

We looked down at our nets. The fish were opening and closing their mouths. They needed water right away!

"I have an idea," I said. "Follow me!"

I ran into the backyard and dashed over to my little sister Georgie's kiddie pool. It was filled with water from last night's storm. I lowered my net into the water. The fish untangled themselves and began swimming around.

"Nice!" said Izzy.

Next, Izzy lowered her net into the pool. The fish swam out of it.

Then we heard a noise. We turned to look. A large van was rumbling up the road.

"That's Officer Pam's van," said Izzy, raising her eyebrows. "Is she here about the fish?"

"Yup! I texted her," I said. "These fish need her help. And if anyone can explain how they ended up on Orange Street, it's Officer Pam."

3 Walking Fish?

Izzy and I walked Officer Pam over to the kiddie pool. We explained how we had found the fish scattered all over Orange Street.

"I'm impressed you girls were able to get all these fish safely off the road and into this pool," she said.

Izzy and I smiled.

I pulled out my notepad. "What kind of fish are they?" I asked.

Officer Pam took a good look at the fish.

"They look like baby striped bass," she said.

"How did striped bass end up in the middle of Orange Street?" asked Izzy.

"That is a great question. I know there are some in the Susquehanna River. And I guess there could be some in Grove Pond, too," Officer Pam replied. "But I have no clue how they got here."

"Do you think the river or pond could have flooded during last night's storm?" I asked.

"You two reporters can worry about all the why's and the how's," she said. "My job is to get these fish safely back to fresh water."

I nodded.

Izzy and I helped Officer Pam lift the kiddie pool into the back of her van.

Then we heard her wildlife radio come on: "Officer Pam! Come to Market Street right away!"

Officer Pam jumped into her van. "Sorry I can't stay," she said. "I'm very busy today since that tornado hit Selinsgrove."

"A tornado?" I repeated. *Last night's storm was worse than we thought!*

"Yes," she said. "The worst of it hit Market Street. Fortunately no one was hurt. But some animals got scared and ran away, so I need to help find them."

"You are the best, Officer Pam," said Izzy.

Officer Pam smiled. "Anytime, girls."

The sun had risen higher in the sky.

I turned to Izzy.

"This is a big day for news!" I said. "A tornado is a huge story. And we need to solve the mystery of how fish ended up on Orange Street."

"Good thing it's still early," said Izzy.

I jotted down some notes.

"Hilde, do you think those fish being in the street could have something to do with the tornado?" she asked.

"I don't think so," I said. "And I don't think the river or Grove Pond could've flooded enough to bring them here. Those are both at least a soccer field away from Orange Street."

"So how did the fish get here?" Izzy asked.

"I'm not sure. Let's head to Market Street," I said.

"Wait," said Izzy. "Which story are we working on? The tornado? Or the fish mystery?"

"Keep up, Izzy," I said. "We're covering *two* stories today. Story number one is the tornado story. We'll cover the storm damage on Market Street. And we'll need to interview Professor Henry, since he chased the storm and knows all about the weather. Story number two is the fish on Orange Street. We need to solve that mystery and —"

Before I could finish my sentence, my nose sniffed the air. "Izzy, do you smell something?"

4 Hilde Versus Tree

Izzy and I ran inside.

Mom was standing over a pan of sizzling bacon.

Izzy turned to me. "Everyone says you have a nose for news, Hilde, but you really have a nose for bacon," she said.

"My belly begins shakin' when I smell bacon!" I shouted.

Then I reached for a bacon strip, but Mom playfully smacked my hand.

"Don't be grabby," she said. "These need to cool off!"

Izzy and I sat down. Our baby sisters, Georgie and Juliet, were watching television. Weatherman Norm was giving a special report about the tornado.

"Look Hilde," said Izzy. "Weatherman Norm is in Selinsgrove! He's on Market Street."

"We need to get over there right away," I replied. "We don't want to get scooped by Norm!"

We jumped up from the table.

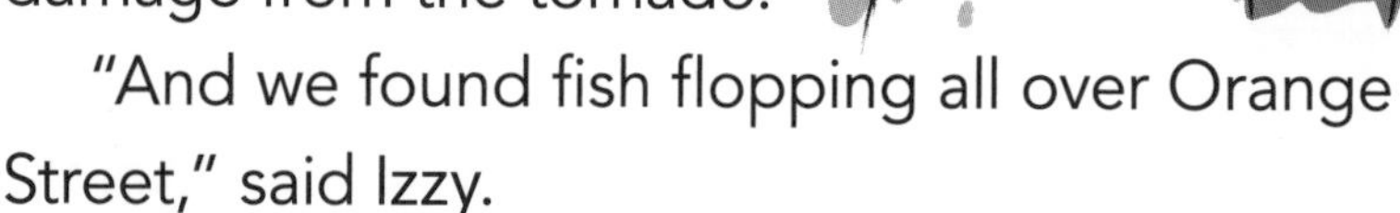

"You girls are always running off," said Mom. "But first, where is my good-morning hug?" She squeezed us in a bear hug.

Izzy and I laughed.

"Mom, we're in a rush!" I said. "We need to cover the damage from the tornado."

"And we found fish flopping all over Orange Street," said Izzy.

Mom turned back to the stove. "Speaking of fish, we'll be having Mr. Troutman's famous fish stew for dinner. Be home by six p.m.!"

"Okay, Mom," Izzy replied.

Before we ran outside, Mom handed us some bacon and two ham sandwiches. I tossed the sandwiches in my tote bag for later.

"Thanks, Mom!" we both shouted. "See you tonight!"

Izzy and I grabbed our bikes. But then I stopped.

"Izzy," I began, "what if the fish were being delivered to Mr. Troutman's grocery store — Grove Grocer — for his fish stew? Maybe a tank fell out of the back of a truck and smashed on the road!"

Izzy's eyes widened. "Let's see if we can find any broken pieces of metal or glass," she said.

I made a note.

We looked up and down Orange Street. There was no sign of a broken fish tank.

"If those fish fell off a truck, the fish tank would have to be here somewhere. Where is it?" I asked.

Izzy scratched her head. "Maybe the truck driver picked up the smashed tank?"

"But not the fish? That would be weird," I said.

Grove Grocer was right up the road. Izzy and I looked at each other.

I checked the time. "It's only six forty-five a.m.," I said. "Grove Grocer opens at seven a.m. So in fifteen minutes, we can ask Mr. Troutman ourselves."

We hopped on our bikes and pedaled toward Pine Street.

There were small pebbles and twigs spread out all the way down Orange Street.

Izzy stopped to take pictures. *Click! Click!*

I continued pedaling, but I called behind me for her to catch up. "Come on Iz —"

Just then, a large maple leaf blew in my face. It stuck right to my forehead!

"Hilde, look out!" Izzy shouted.

I shook free of the wet leaf just in time to see a huge tree lying across the road.

I slammed on my brakes, but I was too late! My front tire blasted straight into the thick tree trunk.

I flew up over my handlebars and into the air.

5 Crash Landing!

I came crashing to the ground face-first into a soft pile of leaves. My front tire had smashed right into the downed tree.

I slowly sat up. Izzy rushed over to me.

"Are you okay?" she said.

"Yeah," I said. I spat a small twig out of my mouth.

"It's too bad they don't make seat belts for bikes, Hilde. Because you could definitely use one," Izzy said as she helped me up.

We both laughed. Then I took a better look at the tree.

"I know Officer Pam said the tornado hit Market Street, but the storm must've been pretty bad here, too," I said, jotting down notes.

Izzy pointed to the bottom of the tree. "Yeah. It looks like a giant grabbed this tree by the top and just ripped it right out of the ground. Check out these roots!"

Izzy took a picture.

She looked at her camera. "I'm getting great pictures for our tornado story."

"Let's try to move this tree off the road so no one else runs into it," I said.

Izzy and I tried to move the tree. But it wouldn't budge.

"It's too heavy," I said.

"We should find Officer Dee and let him know it's here," said Izzy.

Officer Dee was a Selinsgrove police officer. He was also our secret source sometimes.

"That's a good idea," I said. "He's probably over on Market Street."

Izzy checked the time. "But it's seven a.m. now. Should we head to Grove Grocer first?"

"Yes," I said. "Let's go see Mr. Troutman. We need to ask him if the fish we found on Orange Street belong to him!"

6 Market Street Sirens!

Mr. Troutman was sweeping his front sidewalk when Izzy and I pulled up on our bikes. He smiled. "You girls are sure up bright and early this morning!"

"Good morning, Mr. Troutman!" said Izzy.

We dropped our bikes on the wet grass.

I checked to make sure my press pass was dangling around my neck. This way, Mr. Troutman would know I was on the job.

"We are working on a story for the *Orange Street News*. We were hoping you could answer some questions," I said.

Mr. Troutman stopped sweeping the sidewalk. "If you are interviewing people about the big storm last night, I'm happy to say I got lucky. My store wasn't damaged," he said.

"Actually, we were wondering if you are missing any fish?" I asked.

"Missing fish?" repeated Mr. Troutman. He rubbed his fingers through his mustache.

Izzy stepped forward. "Yeah. We found a bunch of fish flopping around on Orange Street this morning. We thought maybe one of your fresh fish deliveries fell off a truck on the way to your store."

Mr. Troutman nodded. "Well, my delivery truck usually gets here first thing, at six a.m. But it hasn't come yet today."

Izzy turned to me, smiling. "Looks like our fish mystery is solved! The tank must've fallen off the truck, and then the driver must've turned back to go get new fish."

But Mr. Troutman spoke up again. "Not so fast, girls. My truck couldn't have spilled your fish. The driver called earlier to say he's running late. He has to take the long way through town, since Market Street is closed," he said.

"Market Street is closed?" I asked.

"Yes," he said. "There are fire trucks and police cars blocking both entrances. No one can pass."

I wrote everything down.

- Mr. Troutman's fish are still on the truck. So the fish on Orange Street were not his.
- Market Street is closed. How bad is the storm damage?

Izzy's jaw dropped. "The damage from the tornado must be worse than we thought!"

I turned to Mr. Troutman. "How bad was the damage over on Market Street?" I asked.

"I was hoping you could tell me," said Mr. Troutman. "You two are the ace reporters!"

I shoved my notepad back in my tote bag.

"We are on the case!" I said.

Izzy and I had just gotten on our bikes when a fire truck raced past us toward Market Street. Its sirens were blaring!

7 Ripped Up by the Root

Izzy and I pedaled down Pine Street. Then the emergency vehicles came into view. Two police cars and the fire truck were there, all with their lights flashing. There was a large yellow barricade blocking off the entrance to Market Street.

A television news truck was parked on the side of the road. Weatherman Norm and his cameraperson were there.

We leaned our bikes against a light pole.

"We need to find Officer Dee and tell him about the downed tree on Orange Street," I reminded Izzy.

"Look! There are more trees knocked over," Izzy said, pointing to two trees lying in the road.

She took pictures.

I took notes.

Izzy and I tried to see more of the storm damage, but the fire truck was blocking our view.

Then we spotted Officer Dee. He stood huddled with Officer Wentworth and Fire Chief Vince. Izzy and I knew all of them from working other stories.

Officer Dee was pointing, but we couldn't hear what he was saying.

"Hilde, why don't you go ask Officer Dee what is happening?" Izzy asked.

I wanted to do just that, but a reporter knows not to interrupt a police officer while they are hard at work.

"He looks busy right now," I said. "Let's do some investigating ourselves. Then we can come back."

Izzy looked around. "There are more trees down across the street," she said.

"Maybe all these fallen trees can help us figure out the path the tornado took last night," I said. "That might even give us a clue about how those fish ended up on Orange Street."

"Good idea," said Izzy.

We crossed the street.

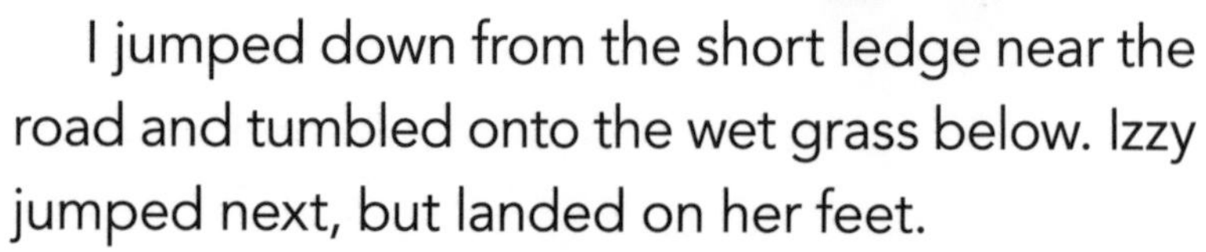

I jumped down from the short ledge near the road and tumbled onto the wet grass below. Izzy jumped next, but landed on her feet.

A long dirt path winded through Selinsgrove Forest.

"Hey," said Izzy. "This is the hiking trail. We've been here before with Mom."

Izzy and I started walking into the forest.

Suddenly, we froze.

8 T. rex on the Loose?

"Izzy, are you seeing what I'm seeing?" I asked.

Izzy lifted her camera. *Click! Click!*

"Trees were thrown everywhere!" she replied. "It looks like a giant ape had a fight with a T. rex."

I had never seen anything like it. An entire row of tall trees had been ripped up, and now they were blocking the hiking trail.

"These trees were ripped straight from the ground, just like the tree I ran into on Orange Street. See their roots?" I said.

"If last night's tornado was powerful enough to tear up *all* these trees, its winds must have been crazy strong," added Izzy.

I examined the ripped-up trees while Izzy searched tornado facts on her phone.

"Listen to this," Izzy began. "Tornadoes have some of the strongest winds on Earth. They can lift trees, cars, and even homes off the ground!"

"I didn't know the wind could be so powerful," I said. "What else does it say?"

"Well, this is surprising . . ." Izzy said. "Most tornadoes only last for about ten minutes!"

"Interesting," I replied.

Then I drew a quick map. I made note of the fallen trees on the hiking trail and the fallen trees along Market Street, plus the one I hit over on Orange Street.

"Keeping track of these downed trees should show us the path of the tornado," I said.

"I'm just so glad no one was hurt last night," Izzy said.

"Me too," I said. "Now let's go see if the emergency workers have finished up. We need to find out what exactly happened on Market Street!"

9 Beep! Beep!

Izzy and I climbed back up the short ledge and walked toward Market Street.

Norm and his news truck had left, along with Chief Vince and the fire truck.

Officer Dee had moved the barricade off the street. A long line of cars and trucks were now slowly passing through.

"Officer Dee!" I called out.

Officer Dee looked up. "Hi, girls!" he said. "I'm sorry, but now really isn't a good time to chat. We had to close this street because the tornado knocked down some trees. I'm here to make sure people can pass safely through town."

A good reporter knows that a little polite persistence can go a long way.

"We understand, Officer Dee, but this is important," I said.

"Really important," added Izzy.

Officer Dee raised his eyebrows. "Is everything okay?" he asked.

"We're fine," said Izzy. "But we found a tree blocking Orange Street and more trees are torn up across the street — on the old hiking trail."

"The hiking trail cleanup can wait, but I'll send someone over to Orange Street right away," he said. "Thanks for letting me know."

"Oh, and there were a bunch of fish all over Orange Street, but we already took care of them," I added.

"*Fish* all over Orange Street?" Officer Dee repeated. He sighed. "Very funny, girls. Now I need to get back to work."

Drivers began beeping their horns.

Officer Dee lowered his eyebrows. That meant he was serious.

"We understand," said Izzy.

"Thank you," we both said.

As we walked away, Izzy turned to me. "What's going on over there?" she asked, pointing.

The fire truck hadn't left. It had moved down the street and was parked in front of my favorite restaurant. Its lights were on!

The Kind Kat Café was the best place to get a quick bite to eat in Selinsgrove. I could see Glenn, the owner, and all three of his cats roaming around outside.

"Come on, Izzy!" I said. "We have a witness to interview!"

10 Shattered Window

Izzy and I parked our bikes in front of the Kind Kat Café.

"Oh, no!" said Izzy. "Look!"

The front window of the café had been smashed and glass was everywhere. The small glass pieces reflected rays of sunlight. The sidewalk looked like it was glowing with white fire.

Izzy lifted her camera. *Click! Click!*

Fire Chief Vince walked over. "I don't want you girls coming any closer," he said. "Broken glass is dangerous. It can cut you."

We nodded. Then we carefully stepped over to where Glenn was standing.

I pulled out my notepad. "Hi, Glenn," I said. "Do you have a minute to talk about the damage to your restaurant?"

"Sure, Scoop" he said. Scoop was Glenn's nickname for me. "I was sleeping when I heard a loud crash. I walked downstairs and saw that a tree branch had come through my front window."

I wrote everything down in my notepad.

"One more question," I added. "I know this sounds strange, but are you missing any fish?"

"Missing fish?" Glenn repeated. "No. And we don't have any fish dishes on the menu this week."

I frowned and looked across at the row of stores on Market Street. I spotted Walter's Books.

"Let's go see Walter," I told Izzy. "Maybe his store was damaged, too."

The bookstore door was propped open, so Izzy and I walked inside.

Walter was sweeping the floor. His upper lip was curled up.

"He looks crankier than usual," whispered Izzy. "You can do the talking . . ."

I walked up to Walter.

"Hi, Walter. We were wondering if your store was damaged during last night's tornado?" I asked.

"Sure was. My sign out front blew off the building. Now I'll have to get a new one," he said.

I took notes.

"Sorry to hear that," I said. "When did this happen?"

"Last night. I was working late. I was sipping hot tea when I heard Glenn's window shatter. The sound startled me, and that's when I dropped my favorite mug. When I ran outside a few minutes later, I saw that my sign was gone," he said.

Walter swept a piece of his mug into the dustpan.

"Is there anything else you remember hearing or seeing during the storm?" I asked.

Walter shook his head. "Not really," he said. "But I'm not the one to ask. Professor Henry stopped in to see if the special book I ordered for him on clouds had come in yet. You should talk to him."

"Yes! We want to talk to Professor Henry," said Izzy.

"Do you know where he went?" I asked Walter.

He crossed his arms. "I'm not his babysitter."

Izzy let out a chuckle. I smiled.

"Thank you, Walter," I said as we left.

I turned to my sister. "Izzy," I said. "I think it's time we talk to Professor Henry. If there *is* a connection between the storm and the fish, he would be the one to know about it."

11 Biting into the Story

Izzy and I grabbed our bikes.

"Do you think Professor Henry is at work?" Izzy asked.

"Probably," I replied. "Let's head to Selinsgrove University and see if he's there."

Just then, my stomach growled.

I checked the time. It was almost noon.

"No wonder I'm hungry. It's lunchtime!" I said. "Let's eat our sandwiches before we head out."

"Good idea! We can review our notes while we eat," Izzy added.

Izzy and I sat down on the curb. I handed Izzy her ham sandwich. Then I took a bite of mine and opened my notepad.

WHAT?

- A tornado
- Fish in the street

(Officer Pam said they're striped bass.)

WHEN?

We found the fish at 6 a.m. But when did they land on the street?

- Trees ripped out of the ground
- Store damage → Broken window at Kind Kat Café → Broken sign at Walter's Books

WHERE?

- Orange Street → Fish were found here → One ripped-up tree
- Selinsgrove Forest → Fallen trees on the hiking trail
- Market Street → Downed trees that blocked traffic → Damaged storefronts

HOW? – HOW DID THE FISH GET ALL THE WAY TO ORANGE STREET?

- Did a delivery truck lose its fish?
- Could the tornado have had something to do with the fish?

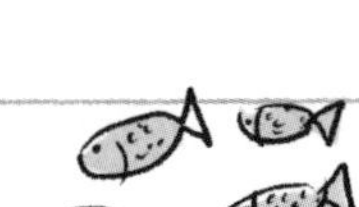

Note: Officer Pam said striped bass live in the Susquehanna River and in Grove Pond. But HOW could they have traveled all the way to Orange Street??

Was there tornado damage anywhere else in Selinsgrove?

Need to find Professor Henry to interview him about the storm!

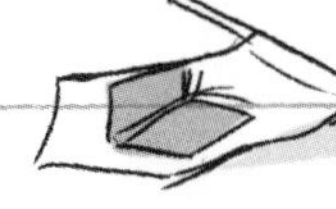

I turned to Izzy. "Remember how Officer Pam said striped bass can be found in Grove Pond? That's a bit closer to Orange Street than the river. Maybe we will find some clues there," I said.

"Great idea," said Izzy. "And we'll pass the university on our way to the pond, so we can stop in to see Professor Henry first."

Izzy and I got on our bikes and headed down Market Street toward Grove Pond. We were passing Rotary Park when suddenly a blanket of brown dust blew up in the air.

I couldn't see a thing!

"Izzy, take cover!" I yelled. "Another tornado is coming!"

12 Surprise Landing

"Hold on tight!" Izzy shouted.

The wind was blowing so hard I could barely pedal. I shielded my eyes and looked around. Then I spotted someone wearing a bright yellow vest.

"There's an emergency worker!" I called out to Izzy over a loud roaring sound.

The worker had a hand raised in the air. In her other hand she was holding a large orange stick.

Izzy and I looked up. The wind wasn't coming from a tornado. It was coming from a helicopter landing in the park!

"What is a helicopter doing in Selinsgrove?" asked Izzy.

"That is a great question," I said.

The helicopter propellers were slowing down. Izzy and I wiped the dust out of our eyes.

"Look," said Izzy. "The helicopter doors are opening."

I could see two men. The first man was wearing dark sunglasses. Izzy and I didn't recognize him. But when we saw the second man step out, we knew right away who it was.

13 Path of Damage

I turned to Izzy. "What is Professor Henry doing up in a helicopter?!"

Professor Henry had a serious look on his face. He wrote something on his clipboard as he walked away from the helicopter.

Now that the propellers had stopped spinning, the emergency worker allowed us to walk into Rotary Park.

"Hi, Professor Henry!" I said, running up to him. "May we ask you some questions?"

Professor Henry seemed deep in thought. Then without looking up, he nodded.

"Why were you flying above Selinsgrove today?" Izzy asked.

"This helicopter belongs to the university, and professors can use it to help them do research. I'm trying to track exactly where the tornado touched down last night. It is easier to see the path of the storm's damage from the sky," he explained. "What have you girls uncovered about the storm?"

Izzy and I told him about all the ripped-up trees and about the fish we found in the street.

"Officer Pam told us striped bass can be found in Grove Pond," I added. "So we were just on our way there to look for clues."

I showed him the map we had made of the tornado's path.

I thought Professor Henry might laugh at my drawing. But he didn't laugh. Instead, his eyes widened!

Then he waved the helicopter pilot over to him.

"Hey, Doug," he said. "Do you have time for another ride?"

The man smiled and gave a thumbs-up.

Professor Henry turned to us. "You girls have given me a new theory about last night's storm," he said. "How about a quick helicopter ride?"

Izzy and I jumped up and down. "Yes!"

"I think you two might have more than a great story. You might have witnessed a very rare weather event earlier today!" he said. "But there is only one way to find out for sure . . ."

14 Flying Reporters

Professor Henry handed us each a headset. Izzy and I stepped inside the helicopter.

We had never been in a helicopter before!

Professor Henry turned to Doug. "Please fly us over to Grove Pond. Then go in a straight line to Orange Street."

Doug gave another thumbs-up.

The helicopter lifted up into the air. Izzy and I gripped our seat belts.

I took out my notepad.

"You said we may have witnessed a rare weather event. What did you mean?" I asked Professor Henry.

"Sometimes when the weather conditions are just right, something called a waterspout can form over a body of water like a pond," he explained.

"What is a waterspout?" I asked.

"It's a tornado that forms over water. And it can lift small creatures out of the water with its strong winds," he continued.

"Small creatures . . . like fish?" I asked.

"Yes, a waterspout can suck up fish, frogs, or other small animals," he answered. Then he went on. "When a waterspout moves over land, it turns into a tornado. And the small animals can stay trapped in the funnel cloud until they fall — like rain — back down to the ground. Waterspouts are extremely rare and unusual, so when one occurs we call it a weather phenomenon."

I wrote down every word in my notepad.

"So if we can find proof there was a waterspout here in Selinsgrove, it would be big news?" I asked.

"Exactly," Professor Henry replied.

"What do you think we'll find at Grove Pond?" asked Izzy.

"Well, if there was indeed a waterspout that picked up fish from the pond and carried them all the way to Orange Street, we should see evidence of damage around the water."

"Evidence like more downed trees?" asked Izzy.

"Exactly," Professor Henry replied. "It should be clear that the tornado started at the pond."

"I see Grove Pond!" I said, looking out the window.

Izzy began taking pictures. She zoomed in for close-up views.

The helicopter circled downward. I looked for signs of tornado damage, but the forest below was thick with trees.

"I don't see any evidence of a tornado here," I said.

Professor Henry turned toward us. "I don't either. The waterspout was a good theory, but I guess it wasn't true. In science — just like in reporting — we need to follow the facts."

I slumped down. I thought we had cracked the case.

Professor Henry was about to ask Doug to turn the helicopter back around when Izzy shouted, "Wait!" She was looking at her camera screen.

Then she called to Doug and pointed out the window. "Can you bring us down a little lower — near that dark green path through the forest?"

Doug pulled down on the throttle. The helicopter dove closer to the ground.

Professor Henry gasped. "Well, I don't believe it!" he cried.

15 Special Report

The helicopter hovered above the edge of the pond. We could clearly see that a group of trees had been ripped from the ground.

"There's our evidence! A waterspout must have formed in Grove Pond! Then when it became a tornado, it went straight through the forest there!" I said.

"Yes! That is what the evidence suggests," Professor Henry agreed. "Now let's see if we were right about the rest of the tornado's path."

He nodded to Doug.

"I will fly us over to Orange Street," Doug announced.

Izzy and I held on tight. My tummy flip-flopped as the helicopter made a sharp turn. Up high, we could see a clear path of damage all the way from Grove Pond to Market Street and up to Orange Street — including the tree that I ran into!

I traced my finger over the spots I'd marked on my map.

Izzy laughed. "It looks like you're playing connect the dots!" she said.

"Science often is a game of connect the dots," said Professor Henry. "And your dots reveal something very exciting! The weather conditions in Selinsgrove last night created a waterspout over Grove Pond, and that waterspout turned into the tornado that hit Market Street!"

"And then the tornado dropped the fish on Orange Street!" I added.

Professor Henry pulled out his phone. "I need to text Weatherman Norm right away. He will appreciate what you girls have found!"

Izzy took more pictures while I typed up my story.

A few minutes later, I felt a slight thud as the helicopter touched back down in Rotary Park.

We all piled out.

"Norm is already here!" Professor Henry said.

Norm was holding a microphone. "Would you two reporters be willing to go live on air? I'd like for *you* to tell the entire state of Pennsylvania what you discovered."

"Sure!" we exclaimed.

The cameraperson stood in front of us. The camera's light went on.

Norm began talking. "I'm live at Rotary Park with two reporters from the *Orange Street News,* Hilde and Izzy Lysiak. They've made a newsworthy discovery."

He passed Izzy the microphone.

"Thank you, Norm," she said. "Last night, there was a rare weather event here in Selinsgrove!"

Then Izzy passed the microphone to me.

"A waterspout carried fish from Grove Pond all the way to Orange Street," I said. "And when the waterspout hit land, it became a normal tornado. The tornado took this path." I held up my drawing of the tornado's path. "The tornado downed trees and damaged storefronts. Then the fish dropped from the sky over Orange Street."

I handed the microphone back to Norm.

Norm thanked viewers for tuning in. The camera's light went off.

"Thank you, girls. Great job!" Norm said. He handed the microphone back to us. "You can keep this for your own video news reports."

"Are you sure?" I asked.

"Yes!" he replied.

"Thank you!" we said.

A car pulled up. Officer Dee called out the window. "You two are on television now?!"

We all laughed.

Suddenly, Officer Dee picked up his police radio. He looked concerned. Then he turned on his siren.

"Officer Dee, what's wrong?" asked Izzy.

"I've got to go! There's a thief on the loose!" he said.

Izzy and I jumped onto our bikes.

"Where are you girls off to now?" asked Professor Henry.

"Wherever news is breaking, the *Orange Street News* is there!" I said.

"Let's go!" Izzy said.

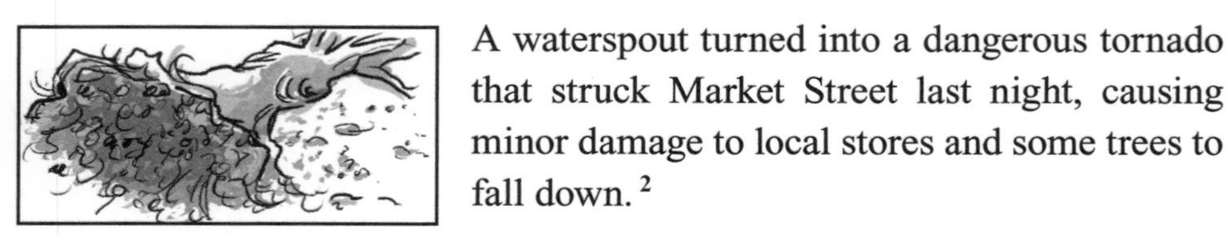

Exclusive!

TORNADO HITS![1]

BY HILDE KATE LYSIAK

PHOTO CREDIT: ISABEL ROSE LYSIAK

A waterspout turned into a dangerous tornado that struck Market Street last night, causing minor damage to local stores and some trees to fall down.[2]

Waterspouts are rare weather events. A waterspout formed over Grove Pond, where it sucked baby striped bass up out of the water. The tornado then traveled down Market Street. Its high winds tore the sign off Walter's Books and uprooted trees — one of which shattered the front window at Kind Kat Café. No one was hurt and no serious damage was reported. Finally, the tornado turned onto Orange Street and the fish fell from the sky.[3]

PHOTO CREDIT: ISABEL ROSE LYSIAK

"The weather conditions in Selinsgrove last night created a waterspout over Grove Pond, and that waterspout turned into the tornado that hit Market Street," said Professor Henry.[4]

Officer Pam collected the striped bass and returned them to Grove Pond.[5]

The *Orange Street News* discovered the weather phenomenon.[6]

1. HEADLINE 2. LEDE 3. NUT 4. QUOTE 5. SUPPORT 6. KICKER

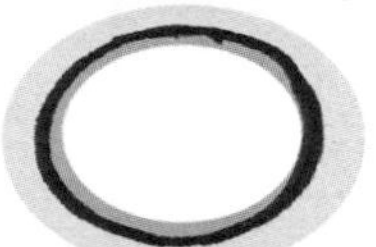

WHO? **Hilde Lysiak**

WHAT? Hilde is the real-life publisher of her own newspaper, the *Orange Street News*! You can read her work at www.orangestreetnews.com.

WHEN? Hilde began her newspaper when she was seven years old with crayons and paper. Today, she has millions of readers!

WHERE? Hilde lives in Selinsgrove, Pennsylvania.

WHY? Hilde loves adventure, is super curious, and believes that you don't have to be a grown-up to do great things in the world!

HOW? Tips from people just like you make Hilde's newspaper possible!

Matthew Lysiak is Hilde's dad and coauthor. He is a former reporter for the *New York Daily News*.

Joanne Lew-Vriethoff was born in Malaysia and grew up in Los Angeles. She received her B.A. in illustration from Art Center College of Design in Pasadena. Today, Joanne lives in Amsterdam, where she spends much of her time illustrating children's books.

TORNADO HITS!

Questions & Activities

1) Wildlife Officer Pam, Police Officer Dee, and Fire Chief Vince help their town after the tornado. What do each of these community helpers do?

2) Turn to the Reporter's Toolbox and find the word *persistence*. What does this word mean? Reread pages 48 and 49. How does persistence help Hilde finish her interview?

3) How does the Kind Kat Café's front window break? Reread page 53.

4) A waterspout hit Selinsgrove! Look up more about waterspouts and other wacky weather.

5) Hilde's map plays an important role in this story. What does your town or city look like? Draw a map of where you live. Label your house and nearby streets.